WHAT
GOOD
WILL
COME

WHAT GOOD WILL COME

by *Jana Hannigan*
Illustrations by Henry Warren

Bahá'í
PUBLISHING

Wilmette, Illinois

Bahá'í Publishing
401 Greenleaf Avenue, Wilmette, Illinois 60091

19   18   17   16   4   3   2   1

Names: Hannigan, Jana, author. | Warren, Henry, 1982– illustrator.
Title: What good will come / by Jana Hannigan ; illustrations by Henry Warren.
Description: Wilmette : Bah?a?i Publishing, 2016. | Summary: When a mishap
   occurs at the Bah?a'?i House of Worship, where a young man named Pasha Dev
   serves as the keeper of people's shoes, Pasha learns the value of prayer,
   fatith in God, and faith in others.
Identifiers: LCCN 2015050636 | ISBN 9781618511034 (hardcover)
Subjects: | CYAC: Bahai Faith—Fiction. | Shoes—Fiction.
Classification: LCC PZ7.1.H364 Wh 2016 | DDC [Fic]—dc23 LC record available at
   http://lccn.loc.gov/2015050636

Illustrations by Henry Warren
Book design by Patrick Falso

DEDICATION

To Hazel, Caixa, Moishe, Orixa, Beto, Katana, Ronaldo, Andrei, Toph, Scout, Ditto, Haji, Supernova, and our stumpy-tailed inspiration who has joined me in prayer many times but would NEVER go out in a storm.

ACKNOWLEDGMENTS

My true thanks to Reed Harvey and Hayden Weiler, whose real-life service at the Lotus Temple planted the seeds of this story, and to Chris Martin, my patient and encouraging editor.

After a long day of driving his taxi in the frantic traffic of Delhi, India, Pasha Dev paused to check the hot glaring sky.

"Rain and fog tonight," he predicted to the searing heat. "See if I'm not right." Then he pushed through the crowded sidewalk and began climbing the stairs to his small apartment.

After washing off the dust and grime of the day, Pasha prepared a simple dinner. He placed two bowls on the table, leaned out the window, and called, "Mustafa! Come for your feast!"

Moments later, a skinny, homely cat streaked through the window onto the floor, purring and rubbing against Pasha's leg. One eye was scarred nearly shut, the other clouded over from some unknown injury, and most of his tail was missing.

"Ah, here is my little Brahmin bull," crooned Pasha, leaning to stroke the cat's back. "All make way for his greatness, Mustafa!"

Delhi crawled with homeless, half-starved animals. They were an unwelcome menace throughout the city. When Pasha came home one day to find a dirty, flea-bitten cat sleeping carelessly in his only chair, he immediately went to shoo him away. But as Pasha thought about the thousands of cars, rickshaws, rooftops, and laundry lines the cat must have navigated to arrive at his second floor window, he felt a Divine Hand must be at work. Instead of casting him away, Pasha determined he would make up for some of the cruelty and indifference in the world by heaping only praise and kindness on this unwanted creature. He named him "Mustafa" —"The Chosen One."

Pasha ceremoniously filled their bowls. "The finest rice and dal for his highness!" he announced. "Surely the Raja himself has not seen its equal," and he chuckled as he watched the ravenous cat empty his dish.

After their meal, Pasha sat in his chair and called, "Come, esteemed effendi. It is resting time. You must rest because that is what royalty does. I must rest because tomorrow is Sunday, my day to serve at the Lotus Temple, and I expect it will be busy as usual."

The Lotus Temple was a popular destination in the capital city. Thousands of people from around the world streamed in every day, and Pasha's duty was to take and return the shoes of all the visitors as they entered this holy place. An entire room was built into the basement solely for storing and managing visitors' shoes. Pasha's job was an enormous responsibility, and he took great pride in the fact that he had never lost or misplaced a single shoe.

"The Temple is like a marketplace of people," he explained as Mustafa, who had heard this speech a thousand times, yawned and made himself comfortable in Pasha's lap. "You can find everything there! Every color, race, and religion. The lowliest beggar. The wealthiest noble. Yet all who cross its threshold, my friend, must surrender their shoes to me."

Mustafa curled up and dozed. "Oh, if you only understood how important my job is, you could never sleep," Pasha continued boasting. "On Gandhi's birthday, the temple had over one hundred thousand visitors! Without me, the temple would have been an unruly disaster, entirely unfit for prayer. That is why they call me the *Shoe Room Warrior*!"

Suddenly, Mustafa woke up and stared keenly out the window. He sat up, craning his head as if hearing a silent call. Pasha looked at him, perplexed. "What is it, friend?"

Just then, a cool gust of wind burst through the open window. A few fat raindrops pelted the glass, then instantly gave way to a smashing Delhi rainstorm.

"Did I not say it would rain?" Pasha shouted triumphantly over the wind. He stood to pull the window shut, but in that exact instant, a small bird, thrown off course by the gale, blew into view, fluttering and struggling to regain its direction. Mustafa, unable to resist, leapt to the window. Guessing his intentions, Pasha cried out, "NO, NO, NO!"

It may be difficult to imagine the swift, brutal violence of a Delhi rainstorm. In minutes, the capital city is brought to its knees as everything becomes a rushing river. Blasting winds tear out trees, rip off heavy branches, and throw them without mercy onto the biggest and smallest of creatures.

At the window sill, Mustafa looked back with his misty gaze and calmly regarded Pasha, who was slipping and stumbling on the already wet floor. For a moment their eyes met. "Please, you mustn't," pleaded Pasha. Then Mustafa sprang after his quarry through the open window and was gone.

"Come back!" shouted Pasha. "You'll be swept away by the rains! Peering desperately into the dark, he searched and called until his clothes were drenched and he stood in a puddle. The storm raged and smashed against the city, but he didn't dare close his window. What if Mustafa should come back?

5

All that night, Pasha slept fitfully under a half-open window, hoping Mustafa would return. And all night the rain spattered in, a cool wind blew over his damp head, and, just as he predicted, a fog settled over the city.

* * *

Achoo! Pasha woke to his own mighty sneeze. The day was dawning as clearly as if it had never heard of rain, and the sky was ready to bake the city again. But Mustafa had not returned, and the worry and chill of the night had left Pasha with a cold.

Pasha lingered at a lonely breakfast, looking for any sign of Mustafa. When he knew he could wait no longer, he set a bowl of food on the table, pushed the window all the way open, and, with a sniffle, left for the Lotus Temple.

Achoo! Through streaming eyes, Pasha saw the temple ahead, rising above the bustling city like a blossom from the mud. *Honk!* He blew his nose as he walked through the long, green temple grounds. *Sniff!* He passed two Buddhist monks spinning their prayer wheels and chanting. *Snuffle!* He stepped around a man prostrating on the steps. *Snort!* Children were cooling their feet in the reflecting pools. *Cough, cough!* Tourists snapped their pictures. *Hack, hack!* He entered the temple, followed the stairs down to the hot, stuffy shoe room, relieved the volunteer on duty, and took his place behind the counter.

Sundays at the temple were particularly busy, and people flowed in steadily, all needing to remove their shoes before entering the prayer hall. As each pair was set on the counter, Pasha gave the visitor a numbered token and placed the shoes in a cubby with the same number. When visitors were ready to leave, they brought their token to Pasha, who found the matching shoes and passed them back to the owners.

With so many shoes, the token system was crucial. *Take shoes, give token. Take token, give shoes.* This was Pasha's graceful dance, and he loved keeping order in the face of such chaos. But today, his mind wandered, preoccupied with worry about Mustafa and dulled by the cold in his head. It was difficult to keep up. His eyes burned, and in the space of a sneeze, ten more people stood waiting for a token.

Lunchtime neared, and the pace quickened even more. Long lines formed, both coming and going. Impatience and frustration grew. His dance became a frantic scurry. Then, at the peak of the noon hour rush and, naturally, at the worst possible moment, Pasha was seized by a fit of sneezing.

ONE! TWO! THREE mighty sneezes!

Please, not now.

FOUR! FIVE!

Oh, where is my tissue?

SIX! SEVEN! EIGHT!

Which pocket, which pocket?

NINE! TEN!

Will this never end?

Several sneezes and tissues later, it was finally over. Exhausted and a little embarrassed, he took a breath, wiped his eyes, turned back to the counter, and then froze in shock! Pasha blinked a few times, trying to focus his eyes and comprehend what he was seeing.

The counter was covered with a mountain of shoes! They were piled so high, they spilled onto the floor. While Pasha was sneezing away, several visitors, both the impatient and the merciful, had simply left their shoes without taking a token.

In a congested daze, Pasha stood staring as seconds ticked by. *But . . . but . . . I am the Shoe Room Warrior.* He tried to reason with himself. *I have never misplaced, never lost a single shoe.*

Still the shoes came. Everyone now was adding their shoes to the pile. Such is the way of people. As he watched this unfolding disaster, something in Pasha snapped like a full sail suddenly cut from its mast.

9

"STOP!" cried Pasha. A raised voice in the temple drew concerned looks. "One at a time, please!" he urged in a hoarse whisper, and with a shove, he pushed all the shoes onto the floor where they scattered like sheep without their shepherd.

Pasha set his jaw, and kept at his duties. *Take shoes.* He forced himself to be vigilant and keep the counter clear. *Give token.* His mind looped in a meaningless drone now. *Take token.* The lunch crowd slackened. *Give shoes.* But the Shoe Room Warrior was defeated, and the unclaimed shoes were heaped at his feet like a monument to his failure.

The day marched into afternoon, and the temperature in the shoe room soared. As Pasha slapped another pair of brown chappals on the counter, he noticed a young woman waving for his attention. She gestured to her feet, speaking some European language. He quickly realized she must be one of the people who had left her shoes without taking a token. This hadn't occurred to Pasha: somehow he would have to match all the unclaimed shoes to the right owners. Things were even worse than he thought! The circles under his eyes grew darker.

As he watched her little pantomime, suddenly all of Pasha's misery and heartbreak found what it was looking for: someone to blame! Anger and even a bit of prejudice flickered toward this stranger. *Tourist.* Pasha scoffed to himself. *She probably wore hiking boots. Tourists ALWAYS come in hiking boots.* He started digging through the pile, making a new mess. *They take forever to lace. Don't they know anything about temples?* But very quickly he spotted two matching hiking boots with long laces. He held them up.

"*Ja! Danke schön!*" said the woman gratefully, but Pasha only tsked to himself and shook his head.

11

As she walked away, a man approached and said, "Sorry to trouble you, but I left my shoes here and now I don't see them." *That's because you are too impatient to follow the rules!* thought Pasha, but then he noticed the man's clean, simple turban. *A Jain,* he thought. *They don't wear leather shoes because they hold all life sacred.* He easily found a pair of rubber sandals.

"How did you know?" laughed the man, incredulously. "Truly, you have a gift."

Pasha shrugged off the compliment, but the man was right. After years of service at the temple, Pasha had seen thousands of different people and twice as many shoes. The time and labor he'd sacrificed had rewarded him with a unique skill: he could match nearly anyone to their shoes. Had he not been so cross, he would have recognized how heroic Pasha the Shoe Room Warrior truly was! But wounded pride consumed his mind, and the pain in his head nailed a scowl on his face.

"Sir?" Pasha heard a reverent whisper and looked up to see an elderly man wearing the traditional aba of a Muslim. "I left my shoes here at the counter, but I'm afraid I don't have a token." Instinctively, Pasha thought to himself, *Muslims remove their shoes five times a day to pray. This man would wear shoes that are easy to get in and out of.*

He sifted roughly through the pile and chose a pair of loafers that looked like they were the right size. The backs had been flattened so that they were more like slippers.

"Yes, these are mine! You are so kind." The man was so courteous and contrite, Pasha had to work very hard to stay angry.

As the old gentleman took away his shoes, Pasha noticed a young girl watching him from a distance, fretting and wiping away tears. Pasha tried to ignore her but finally gave in and waved her over impatiently. Immediately, she burst into sobs.

"Sir, I left my new birthday shoes here, and I don't see them. I think they were stolen!" Pasha easily found her small pair of lovely new embroidered juttis with pink tassels. As she bowed and bowed her gratitude, Pasha felt a bit ashamed of himself for prolonging her distress.

Not much later, he recognized the habit of a Catholic nun coming toward him and quickly found her humble dark shoes with the sensible heels. She was so meek, and her smile was so radiant, Pasha couldn't even look her in the eye.

On it went. As the mountain of shoes wore down, Pasha built up his grudge. Every time he leaned over to fish out another pair of shoes—certain his head would explode!—he silently condemned each guilty party and their shoes: the bride and groom, beautifully dressed, beaming with love, and their fine wedding sandals. The Indian soldier in his fatigues and his army boots. The group of Tibetans and their felt boots with the distinctive toes. The Japanese businessman and his shiny black shoes.

Hindus, Hare Krishnas, Buddhists, Sikhs, Christians, Sufis, Zoroastrians, Bahá'ís, locals, foreigners—Pasha silently tried and convicted each and every one as they were reunited with their shoes until only one pair remained.

Pasha fanned a dim flame of hope. *If I can get rid of this last pair before my shift is over, the person who replaces me won't know anything about this little problem.* Pasha set the shoes on the counter and sized them up: plain brown with just one distinguishing feature—they were enormous!

Simple. Thought Pasha. *I have only to look for a man with unusually large feet.*

Almost immediately, a pair of big feet and bare legs walked toward him. *Here he is now!*

"Sir, are these your shoes?" Pasha called to him.

But as the man came nearer, Pasha saw the red markings on his face, his saffron robes and long hair. He was a Sadhu, one who has given up all worldly things. The shoes couldn't be his.

The Sadhu stopped and smiled. He leaned way down and examined the shoes for a very long time. Then he looked straight into Pasha's eyes. "You are asking the wrong question, my friend," the Sadhu patiently replied. "Your real question is *'Who do these shoes belong to?'*"

The question hung in the air as they stood nose to nose. Pasha, certain that his soul was being searched, flinched and stepped back a bit. Then, the Sadhu suddenly stood up and said, "But I want to say that you are doing a fine job!" He gave Pasha a hearty handshake and shuffled off on his bandy legs.

Pasha glowered. *Perhaps I will become a Sadhu. Then I will never have to see another pair of shoes ever again!* The end of his shift was nearing, and as each minute passed, he grew more anxious, unable to bear the embarrassment of leaving his post with unclaimed shoes. His eyes burned, his head pounded, his body ached, and into the fertile soil of this wretchedness, the seeds of self-pity grew like jungle vines.

Then he remembered the storm. *Mustafa!* For a moment his heart sank. Would he ever see him again? But then he thought, *This is his doing! I treat him like a prince, and he repays me by running into a storm?!*

Then he was angry with everyone who ever came to the temple. *Selfish, impatient oafs who can't wait in a line!*

Finally, in his heartache and woe, he allowed himself the unthinkable. *Why do I bother even coming to the temple? I should sit and do nothing on Sunday like everyone else. What good has come of this? What good?!*

21

It was then that he noticed the hem of a sari and a woman's small, bare feet standing quietly in front of the counter. "Excuse me, sir, but I'm ashamed to tell you that I left my shoes here without taking a token. It was so busy, and you looked so miserable. I hope I haven't caused you any distress." Her voice was gentle. Her face was kind.

"But . . . but . . . are these *your* shoes?" Pasha stammered. Why did he suddenly feel better?

"Yes. They belonged to my father, who passed away recently. I come here to pray for him, and I wear his shoes to feel closer to him. I know I look foolish! But God hears my prayers, not my shoes," and she laughed. It sounded like a thousand silver bells.

Pasha was instantly overcome with relief, gratitude, and . . . something else. He handed the large shoes to this wise, bold woman but took a long time letting go. *What good has come?* He wondered to himself.

When his shift ended, Pasha's nose was still dripping, but he didn't seem to notice. Before climbing the stairs to leave, he took a last look around. Visitors still kept the counter humming, but all the shoes were in their proper places. *And today, the shoes put me in my place*, Pasha said to himself. *I am just a lowly servant, as low as dust on a pair of shoes. Only God is Most High!*

When Pasha returned home that evening, his apartment was still empty. But so was the food dish.

"So, that sacred cow *has* been here!" he said. Elated, he ran to the window and called, "Mustafa! Come for your feast!"

After dinner that night, Mustafa—safe, dry, and well fed—settled in Pasha's lap.

"Beloved, you are most wise. Had you not run out into the storm, I never would have left the window open. And had I not left the window open, I never would have gotten this terrible cold. And had I not gotten this terrible cold, I never would have made a mess of the shoe room. And had I not made a mess of the shoe room, I never would have been humbled. And had I not been humbled, I never would have . . . well, let me tell you about a splendid pair of shoes I saw today, friend."

Mustafa began to purr.

23

During his shift the following Sunday, Pasha watched and waited for the enormous pair of shoes to return. When at last he saw them, his heart quickened! The next Sunday, he learned her name—Kamala. He saw her again the next Sunday. And the next. And the next.

Many, many Sundays later, Pasha was just leaving for the Lotus Temple when he noticed fat rain clouds gathering in the sky once again. He reached outside to shut the windows. "I won't lose you this time, my friend," he said to Mustafa.

"Don't worry, my love," said his wife, Kamala. "Mustafa is more wise and clever than we know. Let's leave them open a bit and see what good will come," and she laughed a laugh that sounded like a thousand silver bells.

Author's note: The Bahá'í House of Worship in Delhi, India—also known as the Lotus Temple—was built for all of humanity. It is a place where people of all faiths and backgrounds come to pray and meditate in their own way or to simply enjoy the peaceful setting. Shaped like a blossoming lotus, the temple's beautiful form and unique purpose draw thousands of visitors every day, often even more than popular tourist attractions such as the Taj Mahal or the Eiffel Tower. On Gandhi's birthday one year, there really were over one hundred thousand visitors!

Managing the shoe room at the Lotus Temple is indeed a big challenge but in reality is done by more than one person. Removing one's shoes at the entrance of a home or sacred place is an ancient custom of respect and reverence practiced in many faiths and cultures. You may even have a friend who does this at home. It is considered a way of making a place more special, a way to leave our troubles of the day behind and enter a place of safety, peace, and love.